Amulet

AMULET
KAZU KIBUISHI

BOOK ONE
THE STONEKEEPER

graphix

AN IMPRINT OF

SCHOLASTIC

NEW YORK   TORONTO   LONDON   AUCKLAND   SYDNEY   MEXICO CITY   NEW DELHI   HONG KONG   BUENOS AIRES

All rights reserved. Published by Graphix, an imprint of Scholastic Inc., *Publishers since 1920*. SCHOLASTIC, GRAPHIX, and associated logos are trademarks and/or registered trademarks of Scholastic Inc.

Library of Congress Cataloging-in-Publication Data is available.
ISBN-13: 978-0-439-84680-6 — ISBN-10: 0-439-84680-3 (hardcover)
ISBN-13: 978-0-439-84681-3 — ISBN-10: 0-439-84681-1 (paperback)

12 11 10 9 8 7 6 5 4 3 2 1   08 09 10
First edition, January 2008
Edited by Sheila Keenan
Creative Director: David Saylor
Book Design by Phil Falco
Printed in China 62

PROLOGUE

WHUD!

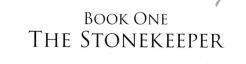

BOOK ONE
THE STONEKEEPER

2 YEARS LATER

IF YOU KEEP THAT UP, YOUR FACE WILL STAY THAT WAY.

I'M TRYING TO CHEER UP 'EM.

SHE'S MAKING THE MOPEY FACE AGAIN.

HEY!

DON'T LISTEN TO HIM, MOM.

I'M DOING FINE.

JUST SO LONG AS YOU BOTH FIND SOME WAY TO BE ENTERTAINED AND STAY OUT OF TROUBLE,

I DON'T CARE WHAT YOU DO WITH YOUR FACES.

ANYWAY, I THINK YOU GUYS WILL LIKE THIS TOWN.

THEY HAVE MINIATURE GOLF.

THE ONLY CATCH IS THAT THIS HOUSE WILL REQUIRE A LOT OF WORK TO MAKE IT COMFORTABLE.

WHY DID WE LEAVE OUR OTHER PLACE?

EVERYTHING THERE WAS BRAND NEW.

UNFORTUNATELY, NEW THINGS COST A LOT.

SINCE YOUR FATHER PASSED AWAY, I HAVEN'T BEEN ABLE TO AFFORD THAT HOUSE.

AT LEAST OUT HERE, WE WON'T BE UNDER QUITE AS MUCH FINANCIAL STRAIN.

THIS HOUSE HAS BEEN IN THE FAMILY FOR YEARS.

MOM, WE'RE OUT IN THE MIDDLE OF NOWHERE.

THERE ARE PLENTY OF PLACES IN THIS COUNTRY THAT ARE OUT IN "THE MIDDLE OF NOWHERE" --

NONE OF WHICH ARE QUITE AS POPULOUS AS NORLEN. IT'S A FAIRLY SIZABLE CITY.

NOW ENTERING
NORLEN
POP. 28,000

YOU'LL SEE. IT'S NOT THAT DIFFERENT THAN ANYWHERE ELSE.

WELL, HERE WE ARE.

SMELL THAT FRESH AIR!

ISN'T IT GREAT?

NOW LET'S SEE IF THESE KEYS STILL WORK.

KLICK

CRUNK

MY GOODNESS...

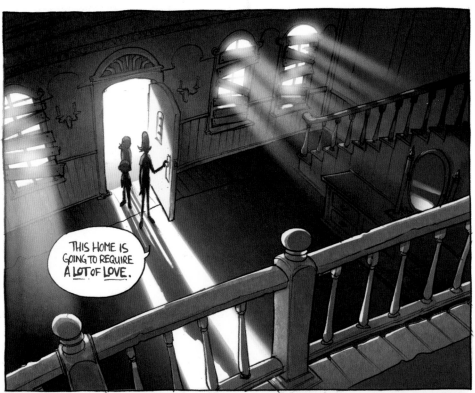

THIS HOME IS GOING TO REQUIRE A **LOT** OF **LOVE**.

EVERYONE STAY CLOSE.

WATCH YOUR STEP.

THERE'S SIMPLY NO WAY WE CAN SLEEP HERE UNDER THESE CONDITIONS.

Sigh.

...WE'LL HAVE TO ATTACK IT.

YOU READY?

READY WHEN YOU ARE, MOM.

BRING IT ON!!!

CHARGE!!!

SHHFF

BDUMP

FSSHK!

SILAS CHARNON

EMILY!

EMILY?

WHOA.

NAVIN!

DISAPPEARED?

AFTER YOUR GREAT GRANDMOTHER ISABEL PASSED AWAY, SILAS LOCKED HIMSELF IN THIS HOUSE AND WAS NEVER SEEN AGAIN.

THIS IS WHY THE LOCALS THINK THIS PLACE IS HAUNTED.

IS IT?

OF COURSE NOT.

GET DOWN FROM THERE!

C'MON, MOM'!

I'LL BE ALL RIGHT!

THERE'S NOTHING UP HERE BUT OLD JUNK!

THERE ARE SO MANY BLUEPRINTS. WAS HE AN ARCHITECT?

NO. SILAS WAS A PUZZLE MAKER. I KNOW HE WAS PROUD OF THAT FACT.

ALTHOUGH, I ALWAYS THOUGHT HIS PUZZLES LOOKED MORE LIKE TOYS OR MACHINES.

CARDBOT

WOW.

YOU SAID GREAT GRANDPA DIDN'T GO TO SCHOOL, RIGHT?

AND LOOK AT ALL THE COOL STUFF HE DID.

EMILY—

MY GRANDFATHER WAS ECCENTRIC.

AND HE'S NOT SOMEONE YOU SHOULD LOOK UP TO.

WHY NOT?

JUST TRUST ME, EMILY. IT'S BETTER TO LEAD A NORMAL LIFE, LIKE EVERYONE ELSE.

NOW LET'S GO DOWNSTAIRS AND FINISH CLEANING.

WE HAVE A LOT TO DO BEFORE IT GETS DARK.

29

SSSHF

I WOULDN'T DO THAT IF I WERE YOU.

WHY NOT?

BECAUSE IT'S CREEPY.

OH, GROW UP.

SHK!

OW!

C'MON EM, WE SHOULD LEAVE IT ALONE AND TELL MOM ABOUT IT.

SHE'LL JUST TELL US TO PUT IT BACK.

HERE, HELP ME PUT IT ON.

I'M NOT GOOD AT TYING KNOTS.

IT'S EASY. JUST MAKE TWO PRETZELS.

CLICK!

THE POWER SHOULD COME BACK ON IN A COUPLE OF DAYS.

UNTIL THEN, IT'LL BE LIKE WE'RE OUT CAMPING.

WHAT'S WRONG, EMILY?

WHY DID WE MOVE OUT HERE?

HONESTLY.

I THOUGHT YOU GUYS WOULD LIKE ALL THIS NATURE.

YOU ALWAYS LOVED SUMMER CAMP.

YEAH, BUT WE ONLY DO THAT FOR A MONTH OUT OF THE YEAR.

NOT, LIKE, FOREVER.

LOOK, I JUST WANTED FOR US TO START A NEW LIFE AND LEAVE THE OLD ONE BEHIND.

I WANTED TO START FRESH. THERE'S NOTHING WRONG WITH THAT, RIGHT?

BUT WE DIDN'T HAVE TO COME ALL THE WAY OUT HERE TO DO THAT.

IT'S NOT SOMETHING DAD WOULD HAVE DONE.

GULP.

WHY DO YOU SAY THINGS LIKE THAT, EMILY?

BUT IT'S THE TRUTH.

LOOK, I JUST—

I DON'T—

36

37

I LOVE YOU BOTH SO MUCH.

I DON'T KNOW WHAT I WOULD DO IF I LOST YOU, TOO.

YOU WON'T.

HOW ARE YOU DOING, EMILY?

ARE YOU WARM?

I'M GOOD. THANKS MOM.

WAIT!

K-THUMP!!

K-THUMP!!

YOU HEAR THAT?

IT'S COMING FROM DOWN-STAIRS.

MOM, WHAT IS THAT?

K-THUMP!

I DON'T KNOW, NAVIN.

CLICK!

YOU TWO STAY HERE WHILE I GO SEE WHAT IT IS.

WE'LL GO WITH YOU.

KRRRK.

I WANT YOU BOTH TO STAY HERE WHERE IT'S SAFE.

IF IT'S REALLY AN ANIMAL, I DON'T WANT YOU GETTING **NEAR IT**.

IT MAY BITE.

I WANT TO GO WITH YOU.

NO.

YOU STAY HERE.

LOCK THIS DOOR IF I SAY SO, OKAY?

MOMMM.

DO AS I SAY!

I'LL BE BACK QUICKLY.

I PROMISE.

SKSSH

SKREE!

C'MON! GET UP!!!

GO TOWARD THE ROCKS!

NAVIN! OVER HERE!

HURRY!

— GRUNT GRUNT

HSSSSSSs.

SNAP!

?

GRUNT
GRUNT

IS IT GONE?

IT'S STILL CLOSE.

WHAT DO WE DO ABOUT MOM?

I DON'T KNOW.

EMILY.

IF YOU WANT TO SAVE YOUR MOTHER, LISTEN VERY CAREFULLY.

MAKE YOUR WAY DOWN INTO THE RAVINE AND FIND THE CAVERN'S CREEK.

FOLLOW IT UPSTREAM TO THE WATER'S SOURCE...

AND THERE YOU WILL FIND A HOUSE BUILT ON A COLUMN OF ROCK.

BEWARE THE CREATURES WHO STAND IN YOUR WAY.

WHATEVER HAPPENS, YOU MUST SEEK THE AID OF THE MAN WHO LIVES AT THE HOUSE...

YOUR GREAT GRANDFATHER, SILAS CHARNON.

NOW GO.

YOU HAVE NO TIME TO LOSE.

WHAT WAS THAT ALL ABOUT?

TAKE MY HAND.

CRUNCH

IT'S A DEAD END.

THE UMBRELLA MUSHROOMS.

PULL THEM OUT BY THE ROOTS AND USE THEM AS SAILS.

SAILS?

WHAT CAN I DO?!

USE THE AMULET.

HWEEEE

PECK. PECK. PECK.

YOU'VE DONE IT ALREADY.

YOU CAN DO IT AGAIN.

NO MORE FEAR.

JUST FOCUS...

AND PROJECT THAT ENERGY...

VRRRRN

WAIT, I MEAN A WITCH. YOU'RE A WITCH.

STOP IT, NAVIN. I'M NOT A WITCH.

BUT THAT WAS SO MAGICAL.

KSSSH!

NOW REMEMBER TO USE THIS POWER WISELY.

BEING A STONEKEEPER IS A RESPONSIBILITY YOU MUSTN'T TAKE LIGHTLY.

A STONEKEEPER?

munch.
munch

munch
munch

EMILY.

DON'T LET NAVIN OUT OF YOUR SIGHT.

HUH?

NAVIN!

NAVIN! GET AWAY FROM THOSE THINGS!!

THEY'RE HARMLESS, EM.

HOW DO YOU KNOW THEY'RE NOT DISEASED?!

C'MON, GET UP.

I CAN'T HAVE YOU GETTING SICK OR HURT NOW.

CHOMP!

FSSSHHHHH

FSHHHHH.

THAT MUST BE THE HOUSE.

WE'LL HAVE TO CROSS.

YOU READY TO SWIM?

NAVIN?

SOMEBODY'S COMING.

SHK!

HUMMM

WHAT IS THAT?

HOLD STILL, AND DON'T SAY A WORD.

SKSHHHH

YOU KILLED HIM!

I ONLY STUNNED HIM.

HUMMMMM

HE'LL GET UP SOON, SO WE MUST HURRY.

TO THE BOAT.

QUICKLY.

WHAT DOES HE WANT FROM US?

THE AMULET.

LIKE MANY OTHERS, HE SEEKS ITS POWER.

AND HOW DO I KNOW YOU'RE NOT AFTER IT AS WELL?

BECAUSE I'M THE ONE WHO HELPED GET IT TO YOU.

IT IS A GIFT FROM YOUR GREAT GRANDFATHER, SILAS CHARNON.

HE HAS CHOSEN YOU TO INHERIT THE AMULET'S POWER.

AND WHO ARE YOU?

I AM HIS ASSISTANT.

WILL SILAS BE ABLE TO HELP US GET OUR MOM BACK?

YOU WILL HAVE THE OPPORTUNITY TO ASK HIM YOURSELF.

UM, HELLO.

SHAKE

NOW PLEASE FOLLOW ME.

IT'S AN HONOR TO MEET YOU, EMILY.

EVERYONE IS WAITING.

EVERYONE?

WHO'S EVERYONE?

HERE THEY COME, RUBY.

SQUEET.

YOU'RE KIDDING, RIGHT?

THEY'RE JUST A COUPLA RUNTS!

HAVE SOME RESPECT, COGSLEY. SILAS KNOWS WHAT HE'S DOING.

I HOPE YOU'RE RIGHT.

DON'T MIND HIM.

HE'S ALWAYS LIKE THAT.

OH, THANK GOODNESS YOU'RE HERE.

OUR MOTHER IS IN DANGER.

THE AMULET TOLD US TO FIND YOU, AND THAT YOU WOULD HELP US.

CAN YOU HELP US?

BUT MY DEAR, YOU MUST UNDERSTAND--

--THAT I ALREADY HAVE.

HWEEEEE

LET ME TELL YOU A LITTLE ABOUT YOUR INHERITANCE.

THE AMULET CONTAINS A STONE THAT CAN GRANT SOMEONE THE POWER TO RULE THE LAND OF ALLEDIA.

ALLEDIA?

IT IS WHERE YOU ARE NOW, AN ALTERNATE VERSION OF OUR PLANET EARTH.

IN TIME, YOU WILL KNOW THE LAND AND ITS PEOPLE.

YOU WILL SEE HOW BEAUTIFUL IT IS.

BUT WHAT DOES THIS HAVE TO DO WITH HELPING US?

THAT WILL BECOME EVIDENT WHEN YOU REALIZE THE EXTENT OF THE STONE'S ABILITIES.

IF YOU CAN MASTER IT,

YOU WILL NOT ONLY SAVE YOUR MOTHER'S LIFE,

BUT YOU WILL GAIN A GREAT AND GLORIOUS POWER BEYOND ANYTHING YOU EVER IMAGINED.

IT IS SOMETHING I FAILED TO ATTAIN DURING MY LIFETIME.

BUT YOU...

YOU CAN ACHIEVE IT.

BUT I'M NOT INTERESTED IN POWER.

I JUST WANT TO GET MY MOM BACK AND GO HOME.

BUT WHAT IF I TOLD YOU THIS POWER WOULD ALLOW YOU TO **TURN BACK TIME**? TO MAKE THINGS GO BACK TO THE WAY THEY ONCE WERE?

THERE MUST HAVE BEEN A TIME IN YOUR LIFE WHEN YOU WERE HAPPIER.

IT'S DIFFICULT FOR ME TO IMAGINE THAT YOU WERE ALWAYS SUCH A SERIOUS AND DETERMINED YOUNG LADY.

YOU CAN HAVE WHAT YOU'RE REALLY LOOKING FOR...

AND ALL YOU HAVE TO DO IS LISTEN TO THE STONE.

IT WILL HELP YOU ATTAIN THE POWER TO SHAPE YOUR WORLD.

IT WILL GIVE YOU EVERYTHING YOU DESIRE, AND MUCH MORE.

I ONLY WISH I COULD BE THERE TO SHARE IT WITH YOU.

EMILY, WHEN I AM GONE, YOU WILL BE LEFT WITH A CHOICE.

YOU MAY CHOOSE TO ACCEPT THE STONE'S POWER OR TO TURN IT AWAY.

JUST REMEMBER THAT EITHER CHOICE COMES WITH GREAT CONSEQUENCES AND SACRIFICE.

BUT WHY? WHY ME?

BECAUSE I KNOW YOU WON'T LET ME DOWN.

MISKIT.

YES SIR.

I LEFT ALL OF MY THOUGHTS AND MEMORIES IN YOUR DATABANKS.

IT WILL BE YOUR JOB TO TEACH EMILY AND LEAD HER DOWN THE RIGHT PATH.

YOU WERE MY APPRENTICE, AND NOW EMILY WILL BE YOURS.

BUT SIR, I'M NOT READY.

YOU WERE BORN READY!

THIS IS WHAT I BUILT YOU FOR.

BUT SIR, I CAN'T DO THIS ON MY OWN.

BUT YOU'RE NOT ALONE.

SO CALM YOURSELF. YOUR FEARS ARE UNWARRANTED.

THE MOMENT I SAW THEIR FACES, I KNEW EVERYTHING WAS GOING TO BE ALL RIGHT.

THAT'S THE FEELING I'VE BEEN WAITING FOR MY ENTIRE LIFE.

IT IS TIME TO CHOOSE.

TAKE SILAS'S PLACE AS KEEPER OF THIS STONE...

AND YOU WILL AWAKEN A FAMILY THAT CAN HELP YOU RECOVER YOUR OWN.

JUST TAKE THE AMULET INTO YOUR HANDS AND ACCEPT ITS POWER.

EM, WAIT.

I DON'T TRUST IT.

WITHOUT POWER YOU CANNOT ATTAIN WHAT YOU DESIRE.

107

THERE MUST BE ANOTHER WAY!

WE CAN DO THIS ON OUR OWN.

HE IS RIGHT.

THERE ARE OTHER WAYS...

...BUT NONE SO CERTAIN.

AND HOW CAN YOU AFFORD TO RELY ON FAITH WHEN TIME IS RUNNING OUT?

YOU KNOW WHAT YOU MUST DO.

EM, NO!

WELCOME
ABOARD,
YOUNG
MASTER.

HWEee····

THEODORE, PUT SILAS IN A SLEEP CHAMBER AND PREPARE HIM FOR TRANSPORT TO KANALIS.

YES SIR.

WE'LL HAVE TO CONSULT THE MAIN COMPUTER TO LOCATE YOUR MOTHER.

PLEASE FOLLOW ME.

EM, I GET THE FEELING YOU'RE GETTING US IN DEEPER AND DEEPER TROUBLE.

LISTEN, WITHOUT MOM HERE, I'M THE ONE IN CHARGE, OKAY?

I CAN HANDLE THIS.

THIS IS A MAP OF OUR CURRENT LOCATION: GONDOA MOUNTAIN.

THE MAP ALSO SHOWS US ALL OF THE LIFE FORMS MOVING WITHIN THE SPACE.

THERE. THAT'S THE CREATURE CARRYING YOUR MOTHER.

IT'S HEADING NORTH TOWARD MORLEY'S CAVE. IF--

SAY IT AIN'T SO, CHIEF!

DON'T TELL ME WE'RE WORKING FOR THESE MUNCHKINS NOW.

EMILY IS NOW OUR CAPTAIN.

SHE'S JUST A KID!

THIS WAS SILAS'S LAST ORDER.

HMPH.

MISKIT, YOU SAID SHE WAS HEADING UP TO MORLEY'S CAVE, RIGHT?

RIGHT.

WELL, THERE'S A TUNNEL THAT COULD TAKE US RIGHT THERE.

WE CAN HEAD THEM OFF BEFORE THEY LEAVE THE CAVE.

THAT'S NOT JUST ANY TUNNEL, KID. THAT'S THE GAUNTLET!

SEE THOSE LIFE FORMS ALONG THE WALLS?

THOSE ARE RAKERS.

WHAT ARE RAKERS?

RAKERS ARE SOME OF THE MOST FEROCIOUS UNDERGROUND DWELLERS ON ALLEDIA.

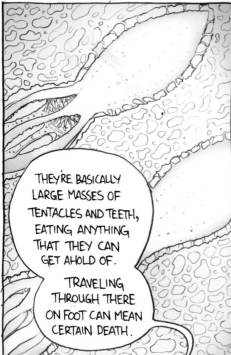

THEY'RE BASICALLY LARGE MASSES OF TENTACLES AND TEETH, EATING ANYTHING THAT THEY CAN GET AHOLD OF.

TRAVELING THROUGH THERE ON FOOT CAN MEAN CERTAIN DEATH.

WHAT OTHER OPTIONS DO WE HAVE?

THE ALBATROSS.

YOU CAN TAKE THE ALBATROSS THROUGH THE GAUNTLET.

BUT THAT JALOPY HASN'T FLOWN IN YEARS!

YOU JUST GET PREPARED FOR TAKEOFF.

I'LL WORRY ABOUT GETTING IT RUNNING.

CAN WE TRUST HIM?

COGSLEY CAN BE A REAL PAIN IN THE BUTT,

BUT HE'S ALSO THE MOST HONEST, HARD-WORKING ROBOT I KNOW.

IT LOOKS LIKE I ONLY HAVE TWO TRANQUILIZER DARTS.

WE'LL HAVE TO MAKE EVERY SHOT COUNT.

WHAT DO WE DO AFTER IT'S SEDATED?

WE **HARPOON** IT AND THEN WE DRAG IT TO A STOP.

POOMF!

THERE.

SHE'S AS GOOD AS NEW.

LISTEN HERE, RUNTS!

MISKIT'S GONNA NEED A CO-PILOT AND NEITHER ME OR BOTTLE HERE CAN GET ABOARD THAT PLANE,

ON ACCOUNT OF US WEIGHING TOO MUCH.

THAT MEANS ONE OF YOU MIDGETS HAS TO HELP FLY THIS THING.

SO WHO'S IT GONNA BE?

NAVIN'S TOO YOUNG.

I'LL DO IT.

WHAT?!

IF I'M TOO YOUNG, THEN SO ARE YOU!

BESIDES, YOU KNOW I'M BETTER THAN YOU AT STUFF LIKE THIS.

BUT YOU'RE TALKING ABOUT VIDEO GAMES.

THIS IS REAL LIFE!

SO?!

EM, PLEASE LET ME FLY THE PLANE.

PLEEASE.

FINE.

REALLY?

ARE YOU JOKERS FINISHED?

120

YER ALL CLEAR! START HER UP!

ERR ERR ERR ERR ER

FWIP FWIP FWIP FWIP FWIP FW

OKAY NAVIN, I NEED YOU TO TAKE THE CONTROLS.

I'M GOING TO REPEL THE RAKERS TO GIVE US A CLEAR PATH.

JUST DO YOUR BEST TO AVOID THE WALLS AND MOVE AS QUICKLY AS POSSIBLE.

VRRRRN

HUMMHNN

THEY'LL BE ATTACKING FROM ALL SIDES, SO GET READY.

HERE THEY COME.

THEY'RE SO SLOW.

WE MUST BE JUST WAKING THEM UP.

IF WE MOVE QUICKLY ENOUGH, MAYBE WE WON'T HAVE TO DEAL WITH THEM.

MISKIT! BELOW US!

128

SPAK!!

GOTCHA!

ARE YOU ALL RIGHT?

I THINK SO, YES.

HEY GUYS—

IT'S GETTING CROWDED UP HERE.

GOOD WORK NAVIN!

CLICK! CLICK! CLICK! CLICK!

KSSSHT!

WE'RE THROUGH THE GAUNTLET!

THEY MADE IT!

HOW FAR ARE WE FROM THE ARACHNOPOD?! OVER!

THEY'RE RIGHT ON TOP OF IT!

YOU'RE RIGHT ON TOP OF IT! OVER!

HE SAYS WE'RE ABOVE IT!

VRRRRN

I SEE IT!

THERE'S MORE THAN ONE! AND THEY'RE MOVING FAST!

NAVIN, TAKE US DOWN.

BUT BE CAREFUL.

HEY LOOK!

140

SKREE!!!

153

SMASH!

LATCH!

KSH!

KSH!

KSH

KSH!

SZRAK!

SKREE!

SKREE!

SKREE!

SPLATCH!!!

MOM!!

LET HER GO!!

I SAID-

LET HER GO!!!

SPLASH!

VWAP!

UNGH!

SKSSSH!

ERGH!

IF YOU WANT THE AMULET, JUST TAKE IT! BUT LEAVE ME AND MY MOM ALONE!

WHAT MAKES YOU BELIEVE I'M AFTER THE AMULET?

IT'S NOT THE STONE I'M AFTER.

IT'S YOU.

ON THE CONTRARY, I WANT TO HELP YOU DESTROY HIM.

IF WE JOIN FORCES, WE CAN FREE THIS LAND FROM HIS IRON GRIP.

AND YOU WILL FINISH WHAT YOUR GREAT GRANDFATHER STARTED.

JUST LEAVE US ALONE.

I'LL MAKE THE DECISION A LITTLE EASIER FOR YOU.

SAY HELLO TO SYBRIAN.

WRAP!

SQUEEZE!

ONCE HE'S INSIDE YOUR BRAIN, YOU WON'T HAVE TO THINK ANY MORE.

NO MORE WORRIES.

JUST RELAX.

NO MORE FEARS.

FEAR...

NO MORE FEAR...

JUST FOCUS...

NO.

YOU'RE MAKING A MISTAKE, YOUNG MASTER.

RUN AWAY.

AND DON'T EVER COME NEAR ME OR MY FAMILY AGAIN. UNDERSTOOD?

Y-YES.

SPLOP!

HUF HUF

ERGH.

EM!!!

173

HER VITAL SIGNS ARE STABLE.

THE POISON WON'T KILL HER BUT SHE NEEDS AN ANTIDOTE.

OTHERWISE, SHE MAY NEVER WAKE UP AGAIN.

URK!

JUST RELAX.

I PROMISED YOU WE WOULD GET HER BACK DIDN'T I?

BUT NOT LIKE THIS!

YOU DIDN'T SAY SHE WOULD BE POISONED!

HOW DO WE FIND A CURE?

SHK!

THAT, MY DEAR, WILL BE UP TO YOU.

SHK!

I'M SO SORRY, MOM.

I'M SO SORRY.

EM, YOU OKAY?

YEAH. SNF. I'M FINE.

KANALIS IS THE NEAREST CITY. WE CAN PROBABLY FIND WHAT WE NEED THERE.

BUT THAT'S THREE HUNDRED MILES FROM HERE.

WITHOUT THE ALBATROSS THAT TRIP MAY TAKE WEEKS.

HEY, DID YOU CLOWNS ALREADY FORGET?

WE'VE STILL GOT ONE MORE VEHICLE.

DO YOU THINK SHE CAN HEAR US?

I DON'T KNOW.

DON'T WORRY, MOM.

EVERYTHING'S GOING TO BE ALL RIGHT.

RIGHT EM?

YEAH.

I THINK SO.

HEY GUYS.

IT'S TIME TO MOVE.

RUBY! THEODORE!

KCHUNK!

MASTERS SECURED! CHECK!

OKAY, BOTTLE. LET'S DO THIS THING.

KDUNK!

BKOOM!

BOOSH!

END OF BOOK ONE

ACKNOWLEDGMENTS

The production of this book was a team effort.

A very special thanks to Alan Beadle, Katy Wu, Arree Chung, Erik Martin, Dawn Fujioka, Dave Au, Sho Katayama, Kean Soo, Sarah Mensinga, Matthew Armstrong, Molly Hahn, Shadi Muklashy and Chris Appelhans for lending a hand in the completion of this book. Without these people, I would probably still be toiling away in a little room, trying to finish it. Most of all, I would like to thank my wife Amy, who painted the colors of many of the pages you hold in your hands, and who has been my biggest inspiration in creating this book.

More thanks go to Taka Kibuishi, Judy Hansen, Sheila Keenan, Janna Morishima, Scott McCloud, Jeff Smith, Ben Zhu, Phil Craven, and David Saylor for their support and patience. Thanks everyone!